Little Book of Princesses

Little Book of Princesses

Buster Books

Contents

What is a Princess?

Princesses are the daughters of kings and queens, but in fairy tales there is a lot more to being a princess than that.

Princesses are expected to keep their promises, to be good and kind, honest and honourable. They have to be true to their principles and true to the men they love. If they are cruel or selfish, they have to learn the right way to behave through suffering and hardship. Only then are they fit to become queens and rule kingdoms.

So being a princess is as much about behaving in a certain way, as it is about having royal blood. The girls in these fairy tales are prepared to risk danger or disgrace in order to behave like a 'proper' princess.

This anthology contains a mixture of popular favourites and less well-known tales, but they all feature princesses who take control of their lives. In *The Magic Fan*, Princess Imani sets out on a journey, disguised as a man, to rescue her love when he falls ill. In *The Wild Swans*, Princess Ellie risks execution to save her brothers from a terrible curse. In *East of the Sun, West of the Moon,* Princess Annalisa risks her life travelling with the North Wind to save the prince she betrayed. Princess Nerys kills snakes, braves the desert and snatches her husband from certain death in the River Nile to cheat fate in *The Prince and the Three Fates.* Few of the princesses in this book sit in a tower, waiting to be saved.

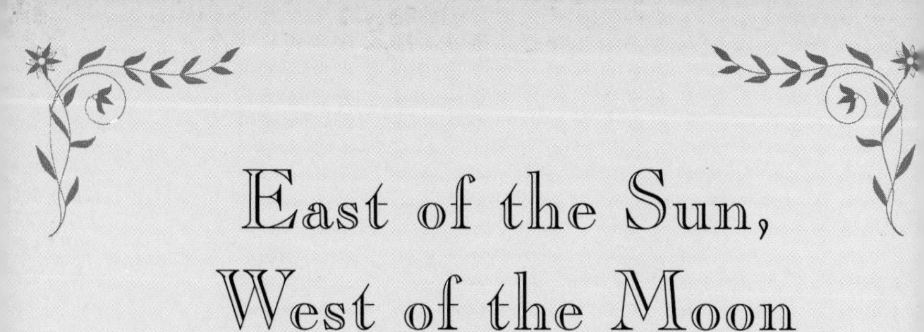

East of the Sun, West of the Moon

Once upon a time there was a king and queen who had six children. Sadly the kingdom was very poor. Neither the royal family nor their citizens had any money.

One evening, the royal family were eating their simple supper. Suddenly, someone rapped on the palace gates. Outside stood a great white bear who asked to speak to the king. The king hurried out.

'Good evening,' said the white bear. 'I would like to marry your youngest daughter, Princess Annalisa, whose beauty is famed. If you agree, your kingdom and all its citizens shall be as rich as it is now poor.'

The king went to tell his family what the bear had offered. Annalisa was horrified at the idea of the marriage, but the king tried hard to persuade her that marrying the white bear would be a wonderful thing for everyone in the kingdom. At last she agreed. When the white bear came back one week later, Annalisa climbed up on to his back.

'Hold on tight to my fur,' said the bear. 'You will be perfectly safe.' And off he strode.

They travelled for many days, until they came to a vast castle made of gold and silver. The bear showed Annalisa to a beautiful bedroom, and then he left her alone. Exhausted, Annalisa climbed into the huge bed. As soon as she put out the lamp, however,

a young man came into her bedroom and lay down beside her. From that day forward, the young man came into the bedroom every night, after Annalisa had put out her lamp. But he always left before daylight.

As the days passed, Annalisa grew sad. The bear asked her why and she told him she missed her family.

'You can visit them,' offered the white bear. 'But promise me that you will never talk with your mother alone. If you do, you will bring misery on both of us.'

Annalisa promised, so the bear took her home. There was great rejoicing. After lunch, the queen begged Annalisa to talk with her alone. Forgetting her promise to the bear, Annalisa agreed. She told her mother about the man who came to her room at night.

'He must be a hideous troll!' cried the queen. 'Take this candle and look at him when he is asleep. But take care not to let any wax drip on him.'

That night, back at the bear's castle, when the young man came and fell asleep beside her, Annalisa lit the candle and looked at him. He was the handsomest prince she had ever seen. She wanted to kiss him but, as she did so, three drops of hot wax dripped on to his shirt. Immediately he sprang up.

'What have you done?' he cried. 'My wicked troll stepmother bewitched me so that I am a bear by day and a human again by night. In a year's time I would have been free from her curse. But now that you have seen me I must leave you, and go to her castle which lies east of the sun and west of the moon. I must marry a troll princess who has a hideously long nose.'

Annalisa begged him not to go, but at dawn, the prince and the castle disappeared and she found herself lying on a grassy mound in the middle of a dark wood.

Annalisa vowed to search for the prince. She walked for days, until she came to a huge mountain, where she found an old woman sitting on a rock, playing with a golden apple.

'Madam, do you know how to find the castle that lies east of the sun and west of the moon?' asked Princess Annalisa.

'No, I don't know the way,' said the old woman. 'But borrow my horse, and ride to my neighbour. Perhaps she can tell you the way. Take my golden apple, it may be useful.'

So the princess rode until she came to another mountain, where an old woman was sitting, combing her hair with a golden comb.

'Madam, do you know how to find the castle that lies east of the sun and west of the moon?' asked Annalisa.

'I don't know the way, but borrow my horse, and ride to my neighbour. Perhaps she can tell you the way. Take my golden comb, it may be useful,' replied the old woman.

When Annalisa came to a third mountain, she found an old woman who was seated at a golden spinning-wheel. The princess asked the old woman if she knew how to find the castle that lay east of the sun and west of the moon.

'Go and ask the North Wind,' she replied. 'Perhaps he knows how to find the castle.' Then she gave Annalisa the golden spinning-wheel, saying, 'Take this with you, it may be useful.'

When Annalisa got to the North Wind's house, she knocked nervously on the huge door.

'What do you want?' the North Wind roared.

'I am looking for the prince who lives in a castle that lies east of the sun and west of the moon. Have you ever been there?' Annalisa asked.

'Yes,' said the North Wind. 'It is an exhausting journey, but tomorrow I will take you on my back, and try to blow you there.'

Next morning, the North Wind puffed himself up, until he was so big and strong that he was a terrifying sight. Away they went, high up through the air. After many hours, the North Wind grew so exhausted that he could hardly blow any more. But at last he dropped Annalisa by the gates of the castle that lay east of the sun and west of the moon.

Annalisa sat down by the castle gates and played with the golden apple. The troll princess, who was to marry the prince, looked out of a window.

'How much do you want for that golden apple?' she asked.

'It's not for sale,' Annalisa answered.

'You can name any price,' said the troll princess.

'Let me spend one night with the prince, and you can have it,' said Annalisa.

'Agreed,' said the troll princess. But when Annalisa went to the prince's bedroom that night he was asleep, for the troll princess had drugged him.

Annalisa called him, and shook him, but she could not wake him. At dawn, the troll princess with the long nose came in and threw her out of the castle.

Annalisa sat down by the castle gate, and combed her hair with the golden comb. Of course the troll princess wanted the comb too. So in exchange for the comb, she allowed Annalisa to visit the prince's bedroom that night.

Again he was asleep, and nothing would wake him.

On the third day, Annalisa sat down by the castle gates and used her golden spinning-wheel. The troll princess wanted it, and the same price was agreed.

Now there were some kindly servants in the castle, who had heard Annalisa trying to wake the prince. They went to him and told him what was happening.

That evening, when the troll princess brought him the drugged drink, he threw it away. When Annalisa went into the prince's room, he was awake. They were overjoyed to see each other and Annalisa kissed his hand softly.

'I am to be married tomorrow, and only you can save me,' said the prince. 'I will vow to marry the woman who can clean my shirt with the three drops of wax on it. Only a human can wash it clean – not a troll. The troll princess will fail, but you will succeed.'

Next morning, the prince said to his troll stepmother, 'I want to wear this shirt at my wedding, but it has three drops of wax on it. I have vowed to marry the woman who can clean it.' So the troll princess with the long nose began to wash the shirt, but the more she washed, the larger the spots grew.

'Give it to me,' said the troll stepmother. But the more she scrubbed it, the blacker the spots grew.

'I'll bet this girl can wash it clean!' cried the prince, and gave the shirt to Annalisa.

'I will try,' Annalisa said. She dipped the shirt in water and immediately it was white as snow.

'You will be my wife,' said the prince.

So angry was the stepmother, that she exploded into tiny pieces, and so did the troll princess. The prince and Annalisa were married, and lived happily ever after.

The Wild Swans

Far away, in a land of endless summers, lived a king who had eleven sons and one daughter. His daughter's name was Princess Ellie. At school the children all wrote with diamond pencils and they read from beautiful picture books that were worth their weight in gold. They were happy, fortunate children, loved and well cared for. But one day, their mother died. In what seemed like no time at all, their father met and married a wicked woman, who became queen.

The new queen hated the children. She insisted that Ellie was sent away to live in a peasant's cottage far from the king's palace. Then she went into the princes' bedroom and chanted a terrible spell.

'Fly away, fly away, fly away.
Become little silent birds, I pray.'

However, the princes were strong, young men, and the magic could only turn them into eleven beautiful wild swans. With a screech, they flew out of the windows of the palace. They flew for two days, crossing a great ocean, until they found a cave.

Ellie stayed with the peasant family and grew into a beautiful young woman. She wept and longed for her brothers, wherever they were.

One day she decided to search for them. For days she crossed fields and moors, until at last she came to a river. She followed the river until it widened to the ocean. She stepped out on to a beach that stretched far into the distance.

As the sun was setting, Ellie sat on the sand looking out at the ocean. Suddenly, she saw eleven white swans, flying towards the land. They flew in a line, one behind the other, like a long white ribbon.

Ellie hid behind some bushes, and watched the swans land and flap their great white wings. As soon as the sun disappeared, their feathers fell off and the swans turned into Ellie's brothers, the eleven princes.

Ellie recognized them immediately and sprang into their arms. The princes were overjoyed to see their little sister again. They laughed and wept, and talked about their adventures.

'By day we are wild swans,' the eldest prince explained. 'But as the sun sets, we turn back into humans again. We live far away, across the ocean, but once a year we come here to visit the place where our mother lies buried. It is a journey of two days, and there is nothing but a little rock rising out of the ocean between here and our cave. We must always be near land before sunset, or we will drown. So at night, while we are human, we have to stand on the rock and wait until morning before we can fly on.'

'Tomorrow we must return to our home,' the youngest brother said. 'We shall not be back for a year, but we cannot leave you here. Perhaps we could carry you across the ocean.'

'Yes, yes!' said Ellie. 'Take me with you!'

So they spent the night weaving a basket with willow and rushes. When it was finished, Ellie sat inside it. As the sun rose and her brothers became wild swans, they took up the basket in their beaks and flew off. They flew high up into the clouds, so Ellie could barely see the waves on the ocean.

The swans were slower than usual because of the weight that they carried. As evening approached, Ellie began to worry, because the little rock in the ocean was still nowhere to be seen. When the sun set, the swans would turn to men again, and they would all fall into the water.

Ellie's heart raced as the sun sank to the edge of the ocean and the swans swooped downwards. She thought they were falling, but they glided on and landed on the rock, just as the sun disappeared into the sea.

The waves crashed against the rock. Ellie's brothers, who were now human again, stood around her with their arms linked together and protected her. At sunrise, the princes became swans again, and flew on.

At last, Ellie spied the land toward which they were heading, with its mountains, forests, towns and palaces. The swans flew to the large cave in the woods where they had made their home.

That night, when Ellie slept, she hoped more than anything to find a way to free her brothers from their spell. In her dreams, a fairy appeared.

'You must knit eleven coats made out of stinging nettles,' explained the fairy. 'You will find the nettles growing around this cave, but if you need more nettles you can only use ones that grow in a churchyard. Gather the nettles with your bare hands and crush them with your bare feet. Use them to make thread with which you will make eleven coats with long sleeves. If you throw these coats over the eleven swans, the spell will be broken. Remember, though, that from the moment you start your task you must not speak. If you say anything at all your brothers will die. Be brave, Ellie.' The fairy disappeared and Ellie woke up.

When morning came, Ellie went out of the cave. Sure enough, she found stinging nettles growing near the mouth of the cave. With her bare hands she picked as many of the nettles as she could find. The nettles gave her delicate hands painful blisters. She bruised her bare feet crushing the nettles, but she was determined to free her brothers. Next, she spun the nettles into thread. At sunset, when her brothers returned, Ellie would not speak to them. She remained silent even though they asked her why she wouldn't speak.

Ellie worked all night and all the next day. She finished the first coat and began the second, but in the afternoon she heard a hunter blowing a horn. Her brothers were not with her and the noise was terrifying. The horn became louder; dogs barked, and Ellie fled into the cave. She quickly tied her nettles into bundles and sat on them.

Suddenly the cave was full of dogs barking loudly. A group of hunters stood outside the cave. One of them, who was definitely the most handsome, was the king of the country. He approached Ellie, because he had never seen such a beautiful girl.

'How did you come here?' he asked.

But Ellie shook her head. If she spoke, she would kill her brothers.

'Come with me,' he said. 'If you are as good as you are beautiful, I will marry you.'

He lifted Ellie on his horse, but she cried because she knew she would not be able to finish the coats.

The king galloped away through the forest to his castle. Ellie was taken to a luxurious room and was dressed in silk. She was treated very well, but she didn't smile once.

One day the king showed Ellie a workroom where he had put her bundles of nettles. On the wall hung the nettle coat she had made.

'Here is your work,' said the king. 'I hope it's what you wanted.'

Ellie was delighted. She smiled and kissed the king's hand. In her eyes the king could see that she loved him. So they were married and all the people rejoiced at their new queen.

Every night, Ellie left the king, and crept away into

the small room. She quickly made one coat after another, but when she began the seventh, she found she had run out of nettles. She decided she would have to find a churchyard and gather more nettles.

The next night, she crept out into the moonlight, and went through the streets of the town until she reached a churchyard. There were terrifying ghosts floating above the tombstones that screamed and tried to frighten Ellie, but ignoring them, she gathered the nettles and took them home to the castle.

Everything had gone well except for one thing – the king's chancellor had followed her that night. He was jealous of Ellie and wanted to turn the king against her. He saw her in the churchyard and told the king.

'She's a witch,' the chancellor insisted.

'Don't be silly,' scolded the king. 'She is innocent.'

But the king began to worry, and wonder what Ellie was doing when she got up in the night to go to her workroom. That night, when Ellie returned to the churchyard to collect more nettles, both the chancellor and the king followed her.

They saw the ghosts, who screamed so loudly that the earth shook. The king went back to the palace. He couldn't bear to think his beautiful queen was a witch. But it was his duty to condemn her to death by fire, the usual punishment for witches.

Ellie was taken to a dark, dreary cell with iron bars. Instead of her luxurious rooms and fine dresses, she was given only the nettle coats she had made to use as a duvet. For a pillow she was given the bundle of nettles she had gathered in the churchyard. Ellie was delighted. She had one more coat to make and only one night left to do it. She started work straight away.

On the day of Ellie's execution, a huge crowd gathered. Ellie was taken to the town square in a cart. But even on the way there, she didn't stop working to finish the eleventh coat. Just as Ellie was about to be thrown into the fire, eleven wild swans flew down. They flapped their large wings, and the crowd was scared and backed away.

As quickly as she could, Ellie threw the eleven nettle coats over the swans. Immediately they were transformed into eleven handsome princes. Everyone gasped in amazement. But Ellie had not been able to finish the sleeve of the last coat, so sadly the youngest prince still had a swan's wing instead of an arm.

'Now I can speak,' Ellie cried, her first words in months. 'I am not a witch. I am innocent.' She told the crowd the sad story of what her wicked stepmother had done to her and her brothers.

When the people understood what had happened, they begged Ellie to forgive them. They lifted her on to their shoulders, and carried her back to the castle and to the king. Ellie's brothers stayed at the castle and they all lived happily ever after.

The Clever Princess

Once there was an emperor who was young and handsome, and very, very ambitious. He dreamed of conquering new lands, and his soldiers followed him gladly. He attacked each of the neighbouring kings in turn and, once they were defeated, he added their kingdoms to his empire.

One kingdom was ruled by an old king named Ivan. Ivan's kingdom was so small that the emperor was too embarrassed to attack it with his huge army. So he chose another way to take it over. He sent Ivan a flock of two thousand sheep and told him to sell them. But, he insisted that Ivan must then return both the money and the sheep to him or lose the kingdom.

King Ivan was in despair. However, his daughter Princess Natasha, who was not only kind and beautiful, but also very clever, told him not to worry.

'Take the sheep to market, and have them sheared. Then you can keep the sheep, but sell the wool to raise the money you need,' she explained.

The old king did just as she suggested. A week later, he took the sheep and the money back to the emperor.

'Who helped you solve my puzzle?' the emperor demanded.

'My daughter, Princess Natasha,' Ivan replied.

The emperor was very impressed, and wanted to test Natasha further.

He ordered King Ivan to bring Natasha to his court in a week's time.

'She must come neither dressed nor naked, neither riding nor walking, neither on the road nor on the pavement, neither bearing a gift nor empty-handed,' insisted the emperor. 'If she can do this, King Ivan, you will keep your kingdom. If not, you will lose the kingdom and your head.'

Anxiously, King Ivan went home and told Natasha what had happened. She smiled confidently.

'Find me a fishing net, a donkey and two hares. Then I will be ready to meet the emperor,' she instructed. So King Ivan did as she asked and a week later, they both set out for the emperor's court.

Outside the palace, a huge crowd had gathered, waiting to see what would happen. When Natasha appeared on the donkey, they saw that she had wrapped the fishing net around her bare shoulders like a huge shawl. She was riding in the gutter with one foot trailing along the ground, and in her arms she held the hares.

Natasha rode up to the emperor and held out the hares. But, as he reached out to take them, she let go of them, and they sped away out of his reach.

The emperor was delighted with the way she had solved his challenge. He marvelled at her cleverness, but he was also captivated by her beauty.

Impulsively he said, 'Princess Natasha, I have never met any girl as clever as you. Will you marry me?'

Natasha looked at him carefully. She thought he was very handsome, clever, and brave, but he was also a bully.

'I could not marry my father's conqueror,' she said.

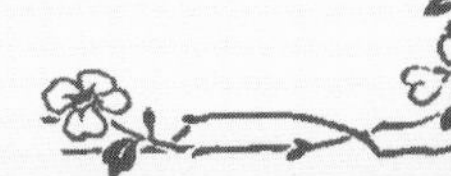

The emperor laughed. 'If I must choose, it is no contest,' he said. 'I'd rather have a clever wife than a bigger empire.'

Natasha smiled. 'Then I accept,' she said.

They were married, and lived happily together for many years. And the emperor always asked his wife's advice before he took any big decisions.

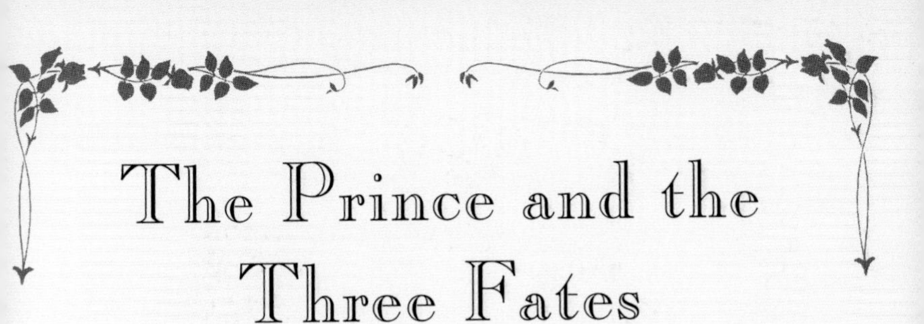

The Prince and the Three Fates

Once upon a time a son was born to a mighty pharaoh who ruled Egypt. The pharaoh was overjoyed at having a child and decided to call him Hassan. He invited all the holy men and women in Egypt to come to the naming ceremony. When the holy men and women gathered around the cradle, the pharaoh noticed they were looking very worried.

'Is there anything the matter?' he asked anxiously.

One wise woman stood up to speak to him. She looked at him sadly. 'Tragically, my lord, we have seen this baby's fate. He is doomed to die,' she said. 'Before Hassan is much older, he will be killed by a crocodile, a snake, or a dog. If we could save him we would; but it is beyond our power.' With this, they left the palace.

The pharaoh was horrified at what he had heard, but he vowed to do everything he could to save his son from his fate. He ordered that a strong fortress should be built where Hassan could grow up safely.

One day the lonely prince was wandering along the walls of the fortress. In the distance, he saw a tiny puppy playing beside the great River Nile. Hassan, who had no friends to play with, fell in love with the puppy. He begged his father to let him keep the dog as a pet. The dog was so small that the pharaoh believed it could not possibly hurt Hassan, so he agreed.

Years passed, and Hassan grew tall and strong. He hated being kept a prisoner in the fortress.

'Why do you keep me shut in here, doing nothing?' he asked the pharaoh. 'I know all about the prophecy, but I would rather die at once than live here. Please let me go to see the world.'

Sadly, the pharaoh agreed. He gave the prince a fine horse, weapons and money, and Hassan rode away with the dog always at his heels. At length his wanderings brought him to another land and another pharaoh's palace. This pharaoh had just built a tower for his only daughter, Nerys. It had seventy floors and each floor had seventy windows. Nerys' bedroom was at the top of the tower.

The pharaoh had sent a servant far and wide to proclaim that any man who could climb up to the princess's balcony would win her for his wife. Everyone had heard how beautiful Princess Nerys was, so many princes came to try their luck. The princess often stood on her balcony, looking down at her suitors climbing the tower. But none of them could reach her.

When Hassan arrived, he was welcomed just as the other princes had been welcomed. Next day, he stood where he could watch the young men climbing, and he noted the places on the tower wall that seemed most difficult to scale.

Day after day he watched, until one morning he felt that he knew which way to climb. So he took his place beside the others and began to climb. He managed to grasp one handhold after another, until at last he stood on the princess's balcony. The people watching from below saw him disappear inside the princess's bedroom.

One of the watchers ran to the pharaoh's palace.

'Sire, the wall has been climbed, and the prize of the princess's hand in marriage is won!' he said.

'Wonderful,' cried the pharaoh, and he ordered that Nerys and Hassan be brought before him. When they entered the throne room, he was so pleased with Hassan's noble air, that he embraced him.

'Who are you?' the pharaoh asked. 'I cannot believe that you are not royal.'

Hassan told him who his father was, and the delighted pharaoh commanded that a wedding should be arranged as soon as possible.

Next day, Hassan felt it was his duty to tell the princess his terrible secret.

'My fate says I shall die young, killed by either a crocodile, a snake or a dog,' he admitted.

'You are mad!' cried the princess, throwing her arms round his neck. 'If you know that, how can you keep that horrid dog with you? Have him killed at once.'

'Kill my dear little dog, who has been my best friend since he was a puppy?' Hassan exclaimed. 'Never!'

However, he promised Nerys that he would always wear a sword, and take a bodyguard whenever he left the palace.

After Hassan and Nerys had been married for a few months, a messenger arrived to tell the prince that his father, the pharaoh, had fallen ill, and longed to see his eldest son once more. So Hassan and Nerys set off to visit him.

When they got there, they were shown to their bedroom. As Nerys lay in the huge bed, she noticed a dark shape in a corner of the room. Gradually, it grew longer and longer, and began moving towards the bed

where Hassan was lying asleep. Then she saw a long, flat head and realized it was a snake. Horrified, she remembered the prophecy.

Nerys slipped out of bed. There was a heavy bowl of milk on a table, which she put on the floor. Holding her breath, she watched as the snake drank greedily. Then she snatched up her husband's sword, and cut off the snake's head. Hassan had escaped the first of his three fates.

A few days later, the old pharaoh died, and Hassan became the new pharaoh. His days were busy and stressful. His one relaxation was to go hunting wild ducks along the banks of the great river. His dog, now very old, always went with him.

On a morning when Hassan and his dog were hunting, the prince tripped over what he thought was a wooden log. But to his horror he saw it was actually a crocodile.

'I am your fate,' whispered the crocodile. 'There is only one way to escape me. If you can dig a pit in the dry sand which will remain full of water, my spell will be broken. You have until sunset tomorrow to perform this task. If you fail, you are mine.'

Hassan walked away sadly. He knew the task was impossible. He shut himself in his room in despair. However, Nerys banged on the door and insisted that Hassan let her in.

'How pale you look,' she cried. 'What is wrong?'

Hassan told her what had happened.

'How can a hole made in sand remain full of water?' he asked. 'The water will seep away. The crocodile will drag me into the river and eat me at sunset.'

'I know what to do,' cried Nerys, embracing Hassan.

'In the desert not far from here, grows a little, four-leaved herb which will keep the water in the pit for a whole year. At dawn, I will go in search of it, and you can begin to dig the hole.'

Princess Nerys was determined to save her husband. She left the palace before dawn and rode away into the desert. It grew hotter and hotter as the sun rose.

After some hours, she saw a tall rock in the distance. The plant grew at the very top of this rock. The stones crumbled away under Nerys's feet as she tried to climb. By the time she reached the top, her hands were torn and bleeding.

There was such a violent wind blowing on top that she was almost blinded with dust. She had to crouch down and feel about for the precious herb. Suddenly, she touched a plant – and it had four leaves! Picking a sprig, she tucked it into her robes and scrambled down as fast as she could. She climbed back on to her donkey and set off home.

When she reached the great river, Nerys ran to Hassan, who was waiting by the pit he had dug in the dry sand. There was a huge water pot beside it. A little way off the crocodile lay blinking lazily in the hot afternoon sun. His jaws, with their sharp yellow teeth, were wide open.

Hassan poured the water into the hole. The moment it reached the top, the princess flung in the magic herb. For half an hour they watched, rooted to the spot, but the hole remained full of water with the little green sprig floating on top. Hassan shouted in triumph, and the crocodile sulkily plunged into the river. Hassan had escaped the second of his fates.

At that moment, a wild duck flew past them.

Hassan's dog dashed after the duck in hot pursuit, and knocked heavily against his master's legs. The prince staggered, and fell backwards into the river. Trapped in the mud and rushes, he screamed for help. Nerys ran to the river's edge and pulled Hassan to shore. Sadly, the poor old dog was drowned.

Hassan kissed Nerys.

'You, my wife, have been stronger than my fate,' he whispered.

The Twelve Dancing Princesses

Once upon a time there was a penniless shepherd boy called Michael. One day, while watching his master's flock, Michael fell asleep under a tree. He dreamed that a beautiful lady appeared to him.

'Go to the castle of Beloeil and you shall marry a princess,' she told him.

When Michael had the same dream the next day and the day after that, he decided he should not ignore the beautiful lady's words. He left his job, said goodbye to his friends and family, and set off for the castle of Beloeil.

Twelve beautiful princesses lived in the castle, but a dark mystery surrounded them. All twelve sisters slept in the same room, and every night their father, the king, ordered his servants to lock and bolt their bedroom door. But each morning, the princesses' satin shoes were found beside their beds, worn, torn and full of holes. When the king asked them what they had been doing all night, they always gave the same answer.

'Only sleeping, father,' they would swear.

In despair, the king proclaimed that the man who solved the mystery of how his daughters wore out their shoes, could choose one of them for his wife. Many princes tried, but each one mysteriously disappeared and was never seen again.

When Michael reached Beloeil, he went to the gardener and asked for a job. His duty was to make the bouquets of beautiful flowers that were given to the princesses every morning. When the youngest princess, whose name was Lina, saw Michael, she let out a long sigh.

'Oh, how pretty our new flower boy is,' Lina whispered. The other princesses laughed at her.

When Michael saw Lina, and looked into her beautiful dark eyes, he decided there and then to try and win her hand in marriage.

That night, the beautiful lady came to Michael in another dream. In one hand she held a laurel tree and in the other, a golden rake, a bucket and a silken towel.

'Plant this laurel in a large pot,' she said. 'Rake it, water it, and wipe it with the towel. When it is as tall as you, say,

My beautiful laurel, I have raked you
and watered you. I have wiped you
with the silken towel.

Then ask for anything you choose, and it will be yours.'

When Michael awoke, he found the laurel tree beside his bed. So he carefully obeyed the lady's instructions. The tree grew and grew. Soon it was as tall as Michael.

'My beautiful laurel,' he said to the plant. 'I have raked you and watered you. I have wiped you with the silken towel. Teach me how to become invisible.'

Instantly, a pretty white flower appeared on the laurel. Michael picked it and put it in his buttonhole and in the blink of an eye, he became invisible.

That night, when the princesses went up to bed, Michael tucked the flower into his buttonhole and

immediately became invisible. He slipped into the girls' bedroom and watched them as they opened their wardrobes, and each put on a magnificent dress and a new pair of satin dancing shoes. Then the eldest princess clapped her hands three times and a secret door opened in the floor.

The twelve sisters disappeared down a staircase. Silently Michael followed. Down they went and through another door into a beautiful wood, where the trees had leaves spangled with threads of silver. Next they entered a second wood with gold-spangled leaves, and followed by a third where the leaves glittered with diamonds.

The princesses walked among the beautiful trees until they reached a lake where twelve little boats were waiting. From a fantastic castle on the far shore came the sound of music and laughter. Quickly, each princess stepped into a boat and sailed across the lake. Unseen, Michael slipped into Lina's boat.

When they reached the magical castle, the princesses went into a grand ballroom filled with musicians and dancers. Michael watched, envying every handsome young man who danced with Princess Lina.

But what Michael did not know, was that these young men were the unlucky princes who had tried to discover the princesses' secret. The girls had given them a magic potion to drink, which made the princes forget who they were. After drinking the potion, the princes never left the castle and lived only to dance.

The twelve princesses danced all night long, until their shoes were worn, torn and full of holes. Then they set off to return home. As they passed through the silver wood, Michael broke off a branch.

He wanted to use it as proof of what he had seen. Lina heard the noise.

'What was that?' she cried.

'It was only an owl,' replied her eldest sister.

Luckily, Michael managed to slip ahead of them. Running up the secret staircase, he reached their bedroom first. He ran to the window, flung it open, and slid down a vine, escaping into the garden just as the sun was rising.

That day, when he made the princesses' bouquets, Michael hid the silver branch in Lina's bouquet. When she found it, she was very surprised and very scared, but decided to say nothing.

That evening, the sisters went to the ball again and Michael followed them. Lina looked everywhere for Michael, but she couldn't see him. As they came back, Michael broke off a branch with gold-spangled leaves. This time the eldest princess heard the noise.

'Sisters, what was that noise?' she asked.

'It is only the cry of an owl,' said Lina.

The next day, Lina found the branch in her bouquet. So she stayed behind.

'Where does this branch come from?' she whispered to Michael.

'I followed you,' replied Michael quietly.

'Oh dear! Please keep our secret,' begged Lina. 'Here is a reward for your silence.' And she gave him a purse full of gold.

'You cannot buy my silence,' answered Michael, and went away without the purse.

The next night, as the princesses returned home from the ball through the wood with diamond-spangled leaves, Lina heard another noise.

Next morning there was a diamond-spangled branch in her bouquet.

'If you reveal our secret you can choose one of us as your bride,' she whispered to Michael.

'I know, Princess Lina,' answered Michael.

'Don't you want to tell the king?' she asked.
But Michael said nothing.

Lina's sisters saw her talking to the gardener's boy. They teased her until she told them that Michael knew where they went at night.

'What?' said the eldest princess. 'A peasant boy knows our secret! He must be sent to the dungeons.'

'No,' Lina declared. 'If you lay a finger on him, I will tell Father our secret myself.'

At last they decided to take Michael to the ball and give him the potion that would enchant him like the other princes. Michael, however, had made himself invisible and heard every word of their plan.

Michael went to the laurel tree, and asked for clothes fit for a prince. Instantly, a beautiful pink flower appeared. He picked it, and found himself dressed in black velvet with diamond buttons.

Immediately, he went to the king, and asked for permission to try the challenge. The king, who was so impressed with Michael's beautiful clothes that he thought Michael was a wealthy prince, agreed to let him try.

That night, Michael went with the princesses to the ball. He danced with each of them, and was so graceful that everyone was delighted. But when he danced with Lina, she mocked him,

'Look at you. You love being treated like a prince. But really all you are is a lowly gardener,' she hissed.

'Don't be afraid, Lina,' Michael replied quietly. 'You will never be a gardener's wife.' And, leaving Lina open-mouthed, he turned and danced with another of the princesses. Lina was surprised to discover that this made her feel very jealous.

After supper, a page brought in a golden goblet.

'Michael,' the eldest sister said. 'You have discovered our secret. Let's all drink to your triumph.'

Michael took the goblet, looked at Lina just once. Then he raised it to his lips.

'Michael, my love, don't drink!' cried Lina. 'I would rather marry a gardener, than lose you.'

And with that, she burst into tears.

In a flash, the potion's power was broken. Michael flung the goblet aside, and knelt at Lina's feet. Each princess chose one of the princes to be her husband, and together they all returned to the castle of Beloeil. As they climbed the staircase to the secret door, they heard a great crash as the enchanted castle collapsed and disappeared behind them.

They went straight to the king and Michael told him what he had discovered. The king was delighted, and asked him to choose his bride. Michael held out his hand to Princess Lina, who blushed and smiled, and took his hand in marriage.

Michael was right, Lina did not become a gardener's wife, because the king made Michael a prince, and they all lived a long and happy life together.

The Frog Prince

There was once a king who lived in a castle with beautiful gardens. In the gardens, there was a deep, cool well. His only daughter used to play with her golden ball beside it.

One day, the princess was in the garden playing, when her ball fell into the well. She sat down and began to cry. Suddenly, she heard a strange voice.

'What is the matter, princess?' the voice asked. The princess looked around her to see who was speaking. Sitting on the wall of the well was a frog.

'My ball has fallen into the well,' she sobbed.

'Don't cry,' the frog replied. 'I can fetch your ball. But what will you give me in return?'

'Whatever you wish, dear frog,' cried the princess.

'Promise to be my friend and let me eat from your plate and sleep in your bed, and I'll fetch your ball,' said the frog.'

'Yes, yes,' the princess promised, not really believing that a frog could live in a castle.

The frog jumped into the well and soon reappeared with the golden ball in his mouth. Delighted, the princess snatched the ball and ran away.

Next day, the princess was at dinner with her father in the great hall of the castle. Suddenly, there was a knock at the door.

The princess went to open the door, but when she saw the frog she slammed it shut.

'What is the matter?' asked the king. 'Is there a dragon at the door trying to carry you away?'

'No!' the princess shuddered. 'Just a horrible frog.'

'What does this frog want?' asked the king.

The princess told him what had happened.

'A promise is a promise,' the king said firmly. 'You must keep it.' So the princess let the frog in. Leaving a trail of wet footprints, he hopped to her chair.

'Lift me on to the table,' he asked. 'Please push your plate over so that I can eat.' The princess did as he asked, but she didn't want to eat any more herself.

When the meal was over, the frog said, 'Please carry me to your bedroom, and let me sleep beside you.'

The princess burst into tears at the thought of sharing her bed with a frog, but the king said, 'You must do as he says.'

Reluctantly, the princess carried the frog to her bedroom. She put him down in a corner of the room. But the frog hopped over to the bed.

'I'd like to sleep on the pillow beside you,' he croaked. With a sigh, the princess obeyed.

The frog slept there all night, but when the sun rose, he hopped out of the palace gates.

'Thank goodness,' sighed the princess. 'Maybe he won't come back.'

But that night, as the court sat down to dinner, the frog knocked at the door again. Once more, he ate from the princess's plate and slept on the pillow beside her. The third night, the same thing happened. No matter how much the princess cried, the king insisted the frog should come in.

The next morning, however, the princess was amazed to find a handsome young prince kneeling beside her bed.

'Dearest Princess, you have freed me from my enchantment,' the prince explained. 'I was changed into a frog by a wicked witch, and I was doomed to stay a frog until a princess let me eat from her plate and sleep in her bed for three nights. You have saved me with your kindness. Now, if you agree, I will love you and cherish you always.'

The princess was delighted and agreed to marry the prince. Their marriage was celebrated that very day, and they lived in great happiness for many years.

The Magic Fan

Once there was a king of Ghazni who had two beautiful daughters – their names were Princess Kupti and Princess Imani. One day, business took the king to the nearby kingdom of Mosul. The king sent a messenger to ask his daughters what gifts they would like him to bring home from his travels.

'A necklace of rubies,' Kupti answered.

But when the king's messenger visited Imani, he arrived just as she was trying to comb out a knot in her hair. Bowing low, he said, 'The king asks what you would like as a present from Mosul.'

Imani, who was only thinking about the knot, replied, 'Patience!' What she meant was that the messenger should wait until she could answer him. However, the messenger left and told the king that the only thing Princess Imani wanted was 'patience'.

'Oh,' said the king. 'I don't know whether I can buy that in Mosul. I never had any patience myself, but if it is possible, I will buy it for Imani.'

Next day the king departed on his journey. When his business at Mosul was done, he bought a beautiful ruby necklace for Kupti. Then he called his servant:

'Princess Imani wants some patience. Go to the market and ask if anyone is selling patience. If you find some, buy it and bring it to me.'

The servant saluted and left the king's presence. He walked about the market for some time.

'Has anyone any patience to sell?' he asked everyone.

At length, Subbar Khan, the King of Mosul, heard about the madman trying to buy patience in the market. The king laughed.

'Bring him here,' he ordered.

When the servant was brought before him, the king asked, 'What are you trying to buy?'

'Sire, my master, the King of Ghazni, ordered me to buy patience,' the man replied.

'Oh,' said the king. 'That's an odd request! What does he want with it?'

'It is a present for his daughter, Princess Imani,' replied the servant.

'Well,' said the king. 'I know of some patience which the young lady might have if she wants it, but you will not be able to buy it.'

The messenger did not realize that Subbar Khan, was making a joke. 'Subbar' means 'patience'.

'Princess Imani is both young and beautiful,' the messenger told the king. 'She is also the cleverest, most loving, and most kind-hearted of princesses. If there is any way to buy patience, it must be done.'

Laughing, the king put up his hand.

'Wait a minute, and I will see what can be done,' he promised.

In his own apartments, he opened a locked cupboard and took out a little casket. He put a fan from the same cupboard into it, and shut it carefully. Then he gave it to the messenger.

'Here is a casket without a lock or a key,' he said. 'It will only open to the touch of a person who truly needs its contents. If the princess opens it she will obtain patience, but I'm not sure if it will be quite what she wanted.'

The servant bowed low and thanked the king, but when he tried to pay, Subbar Khan would take nothing.

As soon as their father got back to Ghazni, he gave Kupti and Imani their presents. Imani was very surprised when she received the casket.

'What is this?' she asked. 'I didn't ask for anything. The messenger left before I had untangled my hair.'

But she took the casket and it opened for her quite easily. Inside there was a beautiful fan. With a cry of delight, Imani took out the fan, and began to fan herself. But she had only made three strokes when suddenly King Subbar Khan appeared before her.

'Who are you?' Princess Imani gasped.

'My name is Subbar Khan of Mosul,' said the king, bowing to Imani. 'You summoned me, and here I am.'

'I summoned you?' stammered Imani. 'How can that be?'

Then Subbar Khan told her how he had heard about a man in his own kingdom of Mosul who was trying to buy patience. When her father's servant told him of Imani's beauty and wisdom, he had decided to send her the fan in the casket.

'Both the casket and the fan are magical,' he explained. 'If you wave the fan three times, I will come to you. If you fold it and tap it three times, I will go home again. You asked for patience – and that is my name – so here I am at your service.'

Princess Imani was very pleased with her handsome visitor, and along with her ladies-in-waiting, they spent a very pleasant evening talking, before Subbar Khan took his leave.

After that, Princess Imani often summoned him.

They were both very fond of chess, and used to sit up half the night playing. Whenever this happened, Subbar Khan used to sleep in the palace and go home again in the morning.

When Princess Kupti heard that there was a rich and handsome young king visiting her sister, she was very jealous. She went to visit Imani. She pretended to be a very loving sister who was interested in the mysterious royal visitor. Imani showed Kupti the bedchamber that Subbar Khan used during his visits.

Later, when nobody was looking, Kupti slipped in to the room. She sprinkled finely powdered glass, which had been soaked in poison, on to the sheets of the bed. Then she made an excuse and left.

That very evening, Subbar Khan came to the palace and sat up late playing chess. Very tired, he said good night. But as soon as he lay down on the bed, thousands of tiny splinters of poisoned glass pierced his skin. He felt as though he was burning from head to foot. All night long he sat in his room suffering the agony.

In the morning, he said nothing and was sent home again via the magic fan. Once he was in his own palace, he sent for all the physicians and doctors in his kingdom, but no-one could cure him. Weeks passed while he tried all kinds of medicines. Soon he was almost dead.

Princess Imani was very troubled. She waved the magic fan again and again, but Subbar Khan did not appear. Every day she waited for him on the roof of the palace. She was afraid that he was tired of her, or that some evil fate had overtaken him. At last Imani decided to go to Mosul and discover the truth herself.

Disguising herself as a young man, Imani set off. On the way, she lay down under a great tree in a forest to pass the night. But she could not sleep for thinking of Subbar Khan, and wondering what had happened to him. Suddenly she heard two monkeys talking in the tree above her head.

'Good evening, brother,' one monkey said. 'What is your news?'

'I come from Mosul,' said the other monkey. 'The news from Mosul is that Subbar Khan is dying.'

'Oh,' said the first. 'I'm sorry to hear that. He is a great hunter and kills the leopards that attack us. What is the matter with him?'

'The birds say that he is dying from the poisoned glass that Princess Kupti spread upon his bed,' replied the second monkey.

'Ah, if they only knew,' said the first monkey. 'The berries of this very tree, soaked in hot water, would cure him in three days.'

'True,' said the other. 'It's a pity that we can't tell someone, and save a good man's life.'

When Imani heard that Subbar Khan was dying, she began to weep silently. As soon as daylight dawned, she gathered a basket of berries from the tree. Then she walked on as fast as she could to the city of Mosul. She went directly to the marketplace.

'Medicine for sale! Who needs to buy my medicines?' she called.

One man said to his neighbour, 'See, there is a young man with medicine for sale. Perhaps he has something that would help cure the king.' He quickly took Imani to the palace.

When Imani entered the sick room, Subbar Khan was so thin and pale that she hardly recognized him. She asked for a room with a fireplace and a pot in which to boil water. Then she soaked some berries in the hot water and gave the mixture to the king's attendants. She told them to wash him with it.

The first washing did so much good that the king slept quietly through the night. On the second day, the king declared he was hungry and called for food. On the third day, he was quite well, but very weak. On the fourth day, he got up and sat upon his throne.

Then he called for the doctor who had cured him to be brought before him.

When Imani appeared, everyone marvelled that such a young man could be such a clever doctor. Subbar Khan wanted to give the young man a huge sum of money and a basket of precious gems. But Imani asked only for the king's signet ring and his handkerchief. She vowed she would accept nothing else. The king handed over the ring and handkerchief. Then Imani left and travelled home to Ghazni as fast as she could.

A few days later, she sent for Subbar Khan by waving the magic fan. When he appeared, she asked him why he had stayed away for so long. He told her all about his illness, and how he had been cured. When he had finished, Princess Imani opened a cabinet and brought out his signet ring and handkerchief.

'Are these your rewards?' she asked, laughing.

Subbar Khan looked at Imani and realized that she had disguised herself as the young doctor. He jumped up, and put the magic fan in his pocket.

'I will never return to Mosul unless you agree to come with me and be my wife,' he vowed.

So they returned to Mosul, where they were married and lived together in peace and contentment.

The Princess and the Pea

Once upon a time there was a prince who wanted to find himself a wife. He was eager to marry, but only a real princess would do. He travelled all over the world looking for a suitable girl. He met plenty of princesses, but he could never be sure whether they were just pretending to be princesses. There was always something that seemed to be not quite right about them.

One day, after many months searching for a bride, the prince decided to return home to his kingdom. He was miserable. The old king and queen were sad too, as they would have liked some grandchildren to fuss over and play with.

One evening, a terrible storm roared around the walls of the palace. There was thunder and lightning, and the rain poured down. Suddenly there was a knocking at the palace gates. The prince sent his man-servant to see who could be calling on such a terrible night.

Outside stood a beautiful girl. She was soaked to the skin from being out in the storm. The water streamed down her hair and clothes. It ran into the heels of her shoes and out again at the toes. The man-servant took her to the king and queen.

'Hello,' she said when she stood before them. 'I have come to meet the prince. My name is Vanessa.

I am a real princess and I'm ready to become his bride.'

'Well, we'll soon see about that,' thought the old queen. She went to prepare a bed for Vanessa for the night. She took all the bedding off the four-poster bed and laid a pea on it. Then she took twenty mattresses and laid them on top of the pea. Then she laid twenty eiderdown duvets on top of the mattresses.

The princess was taken to the bedroom and helped to climb up on top of this strange bed. Then the servants wished her good night and left her to sleep.

In the morning, the queen went into the princess's room and woke her.

'Good morning, my dear. Did you sleep well?' the queen enquired.

'Oh madam, I'm afraid I slept very badly,' replied Princess Vanessa. 'I hardly closed my eyes all night. I was lying on something so hard that I'm bruised all over.'

The queen clapped her hands with glee and rushed out of the room, leaving the princess looking a little puzzled. The prince and his parents, however, rejoiced because now they knew that she was a real princess. She was so sensitive that she had felt the pea underneath twenty mattresses and twenty eiderdown duvets. Nobody but a real princess could be as sensitive as that!

So the prince proposed to Princess Vanessa immediately and they married and lived happily ever after. The pea was put in the king's museum, where it can still be seen to this day.

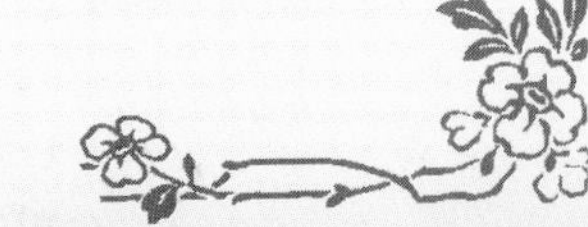

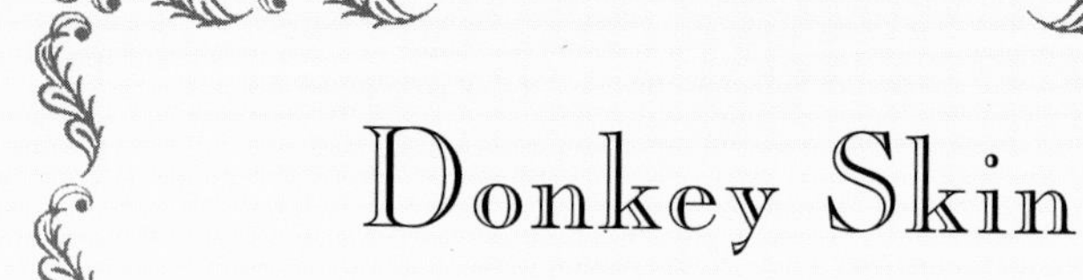

Donkey Skin

Once there was a powerful king who was the richest monarch in the world. He had everything his heart desired, but strangely, his most prized possession was a donkey with large, drooping ears. People did not realize that every night gold pieces tumbled out of the donkey's ears.

Then one day, the queen, whom the king loved dearly, died. The king mourned her for months, but his counsellors begged him to take another wife. At first he refused, but at last he agreed. However, he insisted that the bride should be more beautiful than his last wife. The counsellors sent far and wide to get portraits of all the most famous beauties, but none of the ladies could compare with the late queen.

One day, the king was looking out of the window, when he saw Princess Eleanor. She was an orphan who had been brought to his palace as a baby. He realized that, if a woman existed who was more lovely than his dead queen, it was this girl. At once he asked her to marry him, but Eleanor was horrified and begged for time to consider.

That night, Eleanor went out on her balcony and called to her fairy godmother for help.

'I know about the king,' said the fairy. 'If you don't wish to marry him, ask him for a dress that matches the sky. It's impossible, so you will be quite safe.'

The girl thanked the fairy and went to bed. Next morning, when the king came to see her, she told him that she would not give him an answer until he gave her a dress that matched the sky. The king sent for all the best dressmakers and commanded them to make a dress that matched the sky or he would have their heads cut off.

Dreadfully frightened, they set to work, and in two days they brought back a dress which looked as if it had been cut straight out of the heavens. Eleanor was thunderstruck and begged her fairy godmother for advice. The fairy suggested she should ask for a dress of moonbeams, and then for a dress like sunshine.

The terrified dressmakers made both gowns.

Eleanor's fairy godmother was very surprised.

'You must ask for the skin of the king's donkey,' she cried. 'All the king's wealth comes from that donkey. I am sure he will never give you its skin.'

The princess went to the king and told him she couldn't marry him until he gave her the donkey's skin. The king did not hesitate – the donkey was killed and its skin laid at Eleanor's feet.

The poor girl burst into tears and rushed back to her room and out on to her balcony. She called for her fairy godmother. Thankfully, she came in a flash.

'Wrap yourself in the donkey's skin,' her fairy godmother said. 'Then, leave the palace and go far away. I will look after you. If you stamp on the ground whenever you need anything, you will have it. Go at once – you have no time to lose.'

So the princess wrapped herself in the donkey skin, and slipped out of the palace. The king sent out search parties, but the fairy threw her invisible cloak over Eleanor whenever they came near.

The princess walked for several days, looking for someone who would give her a job to earn her keep. But the donkey skin was so dirty that no-one was interested. At last, she was passing a farmyard when she heard a voice calling her.

'I need a girl to work in the kitchen,' said the farmer's wife. 'Do you want the job?'

Relieved, Eleanor accepted, and set to work in the kitchen. All the farm servants made fun of her at first. They nicknamed her Donkey Skin, but soon they got used to her. She worked so hard, they never guessed she was a real princess.

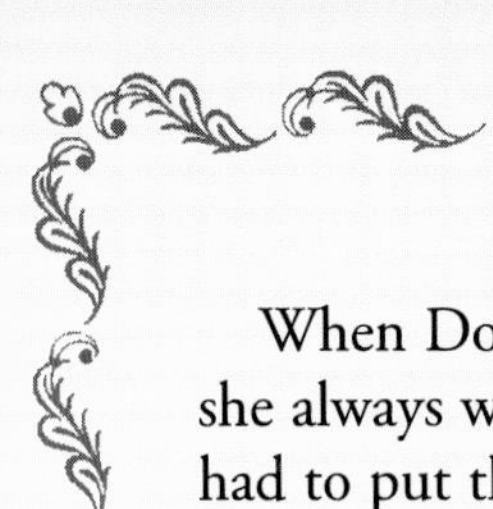

When Donkey Skin went out herding the turkeys, she always washed herself in the stream. But then she had to put the filthy skin on again.

At the end of her first week, there was a holiday. Eleanor rejoiced – for a few hours she could be a princess again. She stamped on the ground, as the fairy had said, and instantly the dress of moonbeams appeared on her bed. She slipped it on and pinned up her beautiful hair in her favourite style.

Now the farm was a royal farm. A prince named Hal had been out hunting and stopped at the farm. Once rested, he decided to explore the house. Eventually he came to a locked door. He peeped through the keyhole and was astonished to see a most beautiful girl in a dazzling dress. When he asked the servants who slept there, they told him it was the kitchen maid, called Donkey Skin.

Prince Hal asked no more questions. He rode off, his head filled with the vision seen through the keyhole. Princess Eleanor saw him leaving and instantly lost her heart to him.

All night long Hal tossed and turned. The next morning he awoke with a high fever. His sudden illness puzzled his doctors. They decided that he must have some secret unfulfilled desire. The queen, his mother, begged Hal to tell her what he wanted.

'The only thing I want is a cake made by Donkey Skin,' he answered.

'Donkey Skin!' exclaimed one of the prince's servants. 'She is the most disgusting creature. She wears a black, greasy skin and works at your farm.'

'Never mind,' said the queen. 'Go to her at once and order her to bake a cake.'

The attendant bowed and sent a page with the message. The moment Eleanor heard the queen's command, she locked herself in her room, tapped the ground and her dress like the sky appeared. Then she took the finest cream, flour and eggs to make her cake. But she added one extra ingredient – an emerald ring from her smallest finger.

When the cake was ready, Eleanor put the skin around her shoulders to cover her magnificent dress and gave the cake to the page. She asked for news of Prince Hal, but the page would not speak to her.

When Hal received the cake, he began to eat so fast that he nearly choked on the ring. Secretly, he slipped the ring out of his mouth and tucked it in his pocket without anyone seeing. The moment the prince was left alone, he took the ring out of his pocket and kissed it a thousand times.

Then he tried to work out a way that he could meet Donkey Skin. He could not admit that he had spied on her through a keyhole. All this worry brought back his fever. In desperation, the doctors told the queen that her son was simply dying of love. Both his parents rushed to their son's bedside.

'Hal, my dear boy,' cried the king. 'Who do you want to marry? You can have her, even if she is our poorest subject.'

The prince showed them the ring, which was an emerald of the highest quality. 'The owner of this cannot be an ordinary peasant girl. I will only marry the girl who can wear this ring.'

The king and queen examined the tiny ring closely and agreed that its owner must be noble, because she had such delicate fingers.

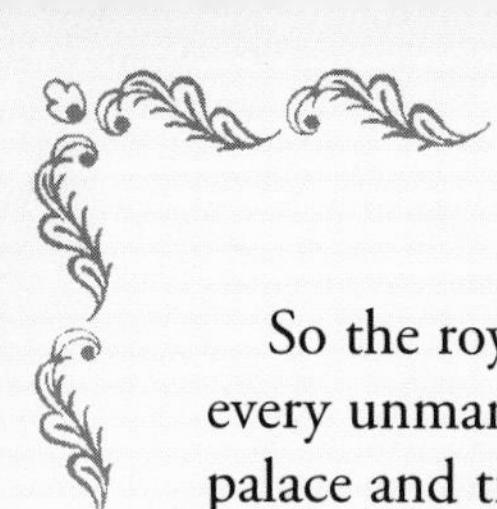

So the royal heralds were sent out, summoning every unmarried girl in the kingdom to come to the palace and try on the ring.

First, all the noblemen's daughters came to the palace, but not one could wear the ring. It was too small. Then the merchants' daughters and girls from the town took their turn, but with no better luck.

'Bring me all the kitchen maids and farm girls,' Hal commanded. But their fingers didn't fit either.

'Everyone has tried, your Highness,' said the chamberlain. But the prince waved him aside.

'Where is Donkey Skin, the girl who made my cake?' he asked.

The courtiers laughed, and replied that such a dirty, lowly creature could not be allowed to enter the palace.

'Fetch her,' ordered the king. 'I commanded every girl to come, and I meant it.'

Princess Eleanor had heard the proclamation. She knew that her ring must be the cause of it and she was terrified that her ring might fit someone else. She dressed herself in the dress like sunshine, then covered it up with her donkey skin, and set off for the palace.

When she entered the great hall in the palace, Hal's heart sank. Had he been mistaken?

'Are you the girl who baked my cake?' he asked.

'I am,' she answered.

'Hold out your hand then,' said the prince, feeling that he must keep his word, whatever the cost.

To everyone's astonishment, a white, delicate hand appeared. The ring slipped on to her finger with the utmost ease. As it did so, Eleanor threw off the black, dirty skin.

She was so beautiful that the prince kissed her hand immediately and begged her to marry him. As he did so, Eleanor's fairy godmother appeared. She explained what had happened to Eleanor and how she had come to be working in the farm.

After the wedding, the king announced that Hal would be crowned king, for he and the queen were tired of reigning. Hal and Eleanor settled down to rule their kingdom and they lived happily ever after.

First published in Great Britain in 2002 by Buster Books,
an imprint of Michael O'Mara Books Limited,
9 Lion Yard, Tremadoc Road, London SW4 7NQ, UK.

ISBN 1–903840–64–3

Visit our website at www.mombooks.com

Picture Credits:
The publishers have made every effort to trace copyright holders. If we have inadvertently omitted to acknowledge anyone, we should be most grateful if this could be brought to our attention for correction at the earliest opportunity.
Anne Anderson 43 (Cope Communications); Edmund DuLac 7, 62; H.M. Brock 26; H.J. Ford 4, 17, 30, 33, 49, 50, 53; Henrietta Wilerbeck de Mare 1 (Cope Communications); Hilda Miller 19 (Cope Communications); Kay Nielsen 9, 11, 14, 36, 41; Millicent Sowerby 3 (Cope Communications); Stanley Woollett 55 (Cope Communications); Stanley Woollett 60 (Cope Communications).
Jacket: Margaret Tarrant (Cope Communications)

Compiled by Clare Charlton
Edited by Philippa Wingate
Jacket and text designed and typeset by Zoe Quayle
Origination by Colourwise Ltd
Printed in Singapore